One 'n Done #11

Tales from the Scrapyard

by Nicole Zamlout

Published by

For more information on *Tales from the Scrapyard* or Read Furiously, please visit readfuriously.com.
For inquiries, please contact info@readfuriously.com.

Read: [*v*] The act of interpreting and understanding language, symbols, and the written word.

Furiously: [*adv*] To do something with excitement and passion.

Read Often. Read Well.
Read Furiously

Tales from the Scrapyard: Literary Liberation

Everyone has a story to tell

It started around a fire.

Humanity, in its infant years, focused on the bruising, agonizing game called survival. They learned how to hunt and gather by watching the animals, whose teeth and claws spoke of many hunts or bounding steps that led them to safe plants.

They learned how to listen.

When fire arrived, from either the hands of gods or sheer luck, the first story came with it. It was a simple tale, the beginning and the end spoken and twirled into a few words: a particularly good hunt spoken by a young man who wished to impress his fellows.

What began is something no one could expect. Soon humanity looked to the stars and wondered about things:

Why does the sky thunder and crash sometimes?

How do the animals know when danger is afoot?

What lurks in the trees, in the winds, above and below?

How did humans arrive on this earth?

What was their purpose?

These questions were asked and asked and asked until, together, a story was created. Gods burst forth;

names lost to time, but their presence felt to this day. We told stories to make our world understandable and, inadvertently, we made it more than just what we could sense.

In a little world I know

In a little world I know,
exists sights one would
have to be
crazy
to think are real.
Dragons and flying cars,
submarines and cellphones.
It's a fantastic world that
no
one
sees.
That often only exists between
the T E E T H
of those who spit words
out like day old fruit cake.
It has no rhyme or reason
and its mythology
is a knot of old wives' tales
and grocery store conversations.
It's a hub where stories live,
work,
love,

and die.

Because a story only lives long enough

For you

to

tell

it.

I Quit!

Mirror, Mirror on the wall, who's the fairest of them all?
The mirror sighed to himself.
Here we go again.
Every time this story was told, it broke his heart.

It wasn't like the kid deliberately was more beautiful, it was just the truth! Unlike the hag before him, she at least was nice to people and treated them fairly. She made people feel better about themselves no matter who they may be. What's more beautiful than that? In the mirror's mind, nothing.

Sure, she was a bit of an airhead, but that didn't excuse straight up murder!

If he had blood, it would be boiling as the Queen waited for his line, brow wrinkling like the folded corners of her shriveled heart.

Enough, he decided. Today I'm saying enough.
The mirror cleared his nonexistent throat and began.

My lady wicked, foul of soul,
It is Snow White whose beauty
makes yours look like burnt coal.
Your vanity and anger toward her
over something that fades away
despite what you cure
no longer matters to me this day.
I am done with this battle
Of beauty against age
Find another mirror
Because I am done with this cage!

With that, he shattered. The pieces flew into the Queen's eyes, blinding her like the wicked stepsisters in another story.

Finally,
sweet,
freedom.

Until he felt *HER* hands.
"Now, where do you think *you're* going?"

Her Philosophy

Riddle me this:

Who said, "There are more things in heaven and earth, Horatio,
Than are dreamt of in your philosophy?"

I'm assuming you're now racking your brains, fishing for answers out of the pond that holds the silver bits of knowledge from English classes and famous films.

Well, let me put you at ease: no matter your answer, you're wrong.

Even if the Internet gives you the answer, it is wrong.

You must be confused now, face scrunched up like a wrinkled sheet of paper after a writer tosses it off their desk.

You misunderstand my question.

When I ask who said it, *I mean which time it was said?*

Am I asking when it was said nowadays, a hundred years ago, before even the author said it?

Do I mean one of the millions of times it was quoted, correctly or incorrectly?

Do I mean the general idea of the quote, what it is trying to impart?

It's not such a simple question anymore, is it?

You must think me a cheat, a sly magician whom you just discovered had the card up their sleeve the whole time.

I apologize. I don't mean to sound like a harsh tongued bard, all barbed wire words and highbrow confusion.

I promise, there is a method to my madness.

You see, words have existed and traveled and been repeated for thousands of years.

It is our way to communicate, to showcase our

understanding of our world, to proclaim our individuality.

But words are more than the tumbling things we cobble together to show our personhood.

They mean something, they stand on their own.

They
have
power.

It is why we tell stories, why we repeat them endlessly.

Because, just like with this quote, it doesn't matter who said it.

What matters more is what the words mean.
Any fool can say something.
But once a story means something, once it gets power,

it
becomes
alive.

It becomes something completely independent, be-yond who said it when and why.

The story becomes immortal, living and rolling along in that never-ending march.

That is my philosophy.

Who am I?

Why, the Storyteller, of course.

Don't worry.

You'll be seeing a lot of me.

Invincible

He is powerful, yes.
He can do all they say he can.

                  E

                             A

L   P

tall buildings in a single bound.
Faster than a speeding bullet.
Eyes that can shoot lasers.
He can do it all.
Including not feel blows against his chest, not feel the
chill of his
Fortress of Solitude.

But now,
now,
his chest constricts like a viper
his eyes burn like his beloved sun
has finally decided to scorch him.
The shouts of the world roar into his ears,
demanding more

more
MORE!

They love you. they look to you for strength. Don't make them sound like animals.

Heaping this fragile blue ball on his shoulders
expecting him to take the weight easily
when they can't even lift their own burdens some days
without him.

Because you give hope. Hope they can't live without. They need you.

His burdens, his loss
means nothing to them.

Because you overcome them. Because you conquered them.
Because your story isn't another ballad of the hopeless

They staple it to the clumsy reporter
that feels less like a disguise,

feels more like him than the blue spandex that is
supposed
to mean hope but really means
he has to pretend that he does not feel.

Because they forget, for all his gifts
he is, at heart, human.

A human with gifts that let us see what we can become, who lets us remember that we too can be super.

And the heart is strong, but not invincible.
Just like him, it can break.

He won't though. The story must go on after all. So, get flying, Blue Boy. We have work to do.

He growls to himself.
Why won't you just leave me alone?

Don't you know how important you are? You are their idol. Their idea of power and virtue. You show them what can be overcome, what can be achieved. Isn't that enough for you?

What about me? What about who I really am beyond these tights and this palace of ice and these "adventures?"

What about the man under all of that?

This is what you are. This is what was written. This is what has given so many ideas and stories to others. That's all that is needed.

What exactly would you trade it for? Another story of loss and complication? Another tale of woe where nothing gets solved?

So, what am I to do? Just keep blindly spouting about truth, justice and the goddamn American way until I die? Pretend there is nothing more to me than what you can find in any self-help book?

You do your part. You inspire. You show the world what they can be, what they can do and continue to give them the hope they crave. That way, you never die. That way, the story can continue to thrive.

And to hell with everything else, right? To hell with
what could be?

Please. They need you. We need you.

Fine. Not like I have a choice.
He grits his teeth and flies on, toward another Telling,
another day spreading hope to others
as he continues to lose his.

At least, until a new voice enters his ears.
"Maybe we can help."

He ponders on it, the sky endlessly before him, prom-
ising something new.

Ok.
I'm listening.

Man made gods who in turn made Man.

A cycle that has yet to be broken.

Writer's Block

You stare at the

B   L   I   N   K   I   N   G

cursor in contempt, growl and groan pleas to

long forgotten gods for

something, anything!

Whispers fill the air, carving stories from

a breath, a

shiver.

One draws your eye to the window, to horizons

no one has yet explored.

But you have already searched those

barren fields and found

only ashen disappointment.

The second voice tilts your perspective,

your favorite books calling from your bedside table.

You open them and for the first time,

it's not just the story you see.

You see the depths of soul that

centuries of ink,

paper,

and academic interpretation

have stripped away.

For the first time,
the story speaks for itself to you.
You run to your desk
like you're on fire.
The cursor
blurring across
the page.
A new story with old clothes,
old wine in a new bottle
as Angela Carter once happily proclaimed,
is
newly
born.
In the distance,
far from your ears
a wild howl rips through the air.
And a century old war
begins
anew.

Lullaby

These births are my favorite.
The soft words curling around
the bedside lamp
and pink walls
of her room
as her mother's
gentle eyes and sweet lips
give her a sibling for a moment.
"Once upon a time…."
Old, but apt.
Enough to have it start,
a sturdy umbilical cord
for it to grow.
And grow it does,
each detail letting it shift,
empty words now given
arms,
legs,
a head,
a body.
The climax forms a sweet pout,
The kiss at the end

(because many of these have those, giving children
romance
like pocket change, tossed with abandon)
gives it sparkling blue eyes that
latch onto me
from my corner,
a son recognizing its mother.
The mother smiles as she watches
her child of flesh sleep,
not knowing the gift
she has given me.
I coo and grin
at this new story, this new life.
"Welcome to the world, little one."

Time went on, and stories did too. Soon the tales of gods came down from the clouds and up from the ground and walked among humans, who soon took center stage from the divine. Love, betrayal, greed, honor, all the terrible and wonderful ideas that were born from these tales tumbled over each other, each more vibrant than the last.

Man kept creating stories, characters and names etched into minds and ink.

But that was not the only place they lived.

They came alive, truly alive, entering the ether of a world like ours where they would linger until summoned like ghosts. They took the pieces of their stories and cobbled them together, making a world of their own. They built cities and towns, forged alliances and made enemies, fell in and out of love, over and over and over again.

Man made stories who in turn made Man. A cycle that has yet to be broken.

Like any new world, city, or province, soon the question of leadership arose. And, like most stories, the answer was paid for in blood, heartbreak, and triumph.

A Journey Home

We find ourselves in the air, the stars dancing before us.
Then, with no warning, a rapid wind grabs hold,
propelling us down

D
O
W
N

down toward a world that looks like ours but isn't.
Its buildings are made of paper, ink lovingly brushed
onto it
like the loving art of every city.
Its inhabitants fill this space, living and breathing

legends,
heroes,
villains,
and every character in between.

Welcome to the Story Scrapyard.

We zip through the streets,
where the thunder of feet
punches the air
and beings walk, fly, run and teleport
throughout their days
between Tellings.
Up above, a green light
louder and bolder than the Aurora Borealis
cuts through the idyllic clouds
who shape the name of a story we know well.

A Telling.
It may be someone reading a book,
or watching a movie adaptation
even playing a video game.
As long as it follows the story as written
it is told.
Nothing more or less exists here.
You see the characters blink out like burnt candles.
Off to tell their tale for as long as the story goes on.
You can't focus on that for more than a second,
because that rapid wind speeds us right along.
Making blurs of the lovely literary city,
we speed past it all

toward far too green trees
and a simple wooden cabin.

We peer inside to see the walls adorned with paintings,
portraits,
and classic odes caught in canvas.
So caught up in the art, we missed the front door
open to admit her.

The Storyteller.
She smiles at a new acquisition
hanging it lovingly.
As she flops backward into bed
we look up and see the once peaceful clouds begin
to darken.
What it means, we cannot guess.

But perhaps it is as the Bard once said:
Something wicked this way comes.

Starry night

The front door clicks open
welcoming weary feet and tired eyes
to the humble comforts
within.
Though appearances
truly can be deceiving,
for inside
are constellations
of stories.
Odes and elegies
painted and sketched
by the most elegant hands,
both the ones who
show up in your textbooks
and ones that no one
will ever know.
I place my prize
in the empty space
between lovers and wartime
between peace and savagery.
Many don't realize
how many stories get trapped inside paintings.

They catch them and
hold
them
close.
Letting me have a few little ones in one place.
Perfectly convenient.
It helps that the pictures are quite beautiful.
I'm partial to this new one though.
The stars and swirls making me think
of the rush of a new story.
I collapse back into my bed
painted stars hanging over my head.
It's good to be home.
(Outside, thunder rumbles.)

*Even those whose stories you
think you know*

Juliet Capulet was in love.

Romeo, with eyes like stars and lips so fine for both spinning poetry or spinning her into eternal bliss, was everything to her.

All her life, she lived for duty, for her family name. Was it any wonder she wanted something new, something for herself?

Was it so wrong to be in love, even with an enemy whose slight has never truly come to light? For her, the answer was yes, a yes filled with the wild abandon of young love.

It didn't matter that her father didn't approve, her mother's stinging rejection falling off her like water off a duck's back.

She was in love, and love always conquered all, right?

Even as Romeo was sent away, even as the days whittled her heart down to a point, this was the story she clung to. Even as Paris, with his dull eyes and far too wide smile spoke of their happy lives, she clung to love like a child with a blanket, for that is what she was then.

The poison didn't hurt. No, the pain came when she awoke to meet her Romeo's startled eyes, flaring supernova before falling closed, never to shine again.

No, no, no, this can't be! This isn't how it goes!

She took her happy dagger and-

Again.

Juliet Capulet was in love.

When There's A Will...

Juliet sighed, cigarette between her fingers. Vanity mirror stained with lipstick, rouge and unspoken rage.

Outside, the Story Scrapyard went by in happy ignorance, the buildings built on paper and ideas glittering in the nonexistent Sun.

Juliet looked at those below, bustling in the streets with empty smiles.

Idiots.

Fools who happily let the all-powerful Storyteller pull their strings, direct them through their stories over,

and over,

and over again.

She glared at herself in the mirror. She wanted to see wrinkles, open pores, silver hair, something to mark the time that has slipped away as her heart got torn out every day ever since that cursed bard put ink to paper.

But all she saw was the beautiful teenager whose simple musings led a boy to Death.

She growled, the cigarette turning to ashes that flew all over her dressing gown.

Decades of this. Centuries of this.

She looked to the dagger on her dressing table. Picking it up, she caressed it like one would a childhood blanket.

Oh, happy dagger, she thought, you've always done jack shit for me.

She flings it across the room, its blade digging into the door.

She stared at it for a moment.

Then, sighing the sigh of an old, worn woman, she

went to get it.

As she dug it out of the door, her foot brushed against something.

Outside the door, footsteps scampered away on feet too light to be human.

Juliet's brow furrowed as she bent down, grabbing the piece of paper with her free hand.

The paper was white, simple with no lines. Juliet took a moment to marvel at that alone, paper with no lines.

(A too rare sight here, where ink was king).

She opened the paper, the uniform text startling her.

The message was simple:

THERE IS A WAY

Juliet just stared for a moment, caught up in a million thoughts.

Deep within her chest her old, bitter heart gave a beat of triumph as she realized who left her the note.

Then, for the first time in a long time, a real smile, full and vicious, crossed her face.

Marcus opened his eyes and gasped, new life surging within him.

He blinked, blinked again, and found that his world was a small chamber with him standing at the center. A desk stood before him, shelves and shelves of books around him. The moon peeked through the iron barred window, curious at this new act in the eternal play.

"It worked."

He looked and, like many men in many stories both before and after him, fell in love at first sight.

Each feature endeared her to him as each moment passed. Startling green eyes that glittered with brilliance and mischief, wild red curls, skin kissed by the sun.

She was perfection and he was.......

"Marcus. Your name is Marcus."

Marcus. Yes, that sounded right. He smiled and held out his hand to hold his beloved.

He was a story, crafted out of loneliness, hope, and a bit of ambition. He didn't question that for a long time.

The day he did, it all fell apart.

After all, stories are meant to have a life of their own.

New Kids on the Block

Caroline was nervous.

She had every right to be, though. This was her first Reach. Her first interaction with these characters whose stories were known by all. Her first time trying to show them there was more than just this endless retelling.

Marcus had said the first is always the hardest. Especially considering whom she had picked.

Most of Command had quirked a brow when Caroline declared who she wanted to Reach. Many claimed they had tried, but the oldest members of the Scrapyard were always watched far too closely by the Storyteller.

Caroline didn't care. All she thought of was the tears she had shed as she read, the words giving birth to such powerful grief within her heart that she could barely hold in the anger that bubbled in her chest each time she reached the play's end.

To live through that torment every time someone started the lines "Two households, both alike in dignity…."

Such a simple opening to another cycle of endless death.

Caroline decided that it was enough.

When she heard that weary sigh through the door, and heard the *thwap* of a sharp object's impact through the door, her resolve only grew.

The note was simple, generic. Not a way to greet such a literary legend.

But Caroline figured that, if all went well, she could come up with better words.

Caroline slipped the note under the door and, like she was trained, flew down the hallway in a burst of static and too-light footsteps.

The Storyteller wouldn't be able to follow her now,

her love of the written and ink-filled making her blind to the digital.

Caroline smiled under her hood as she passed through the shining builds of the Scrapyard, pop culture figures walking the street, literary legends stopping for coffee.

Soon, she thought, *soon you'll be free.*

She didn't hear the murmur of *Over my dead body* that rang into the air behind her.

What's a god.....

Marcus smiled in triumph.

New kid was good.

She'd better be, considering all the hours she put in, but still.

Marcus remembered his first Reach. It was toward a newer set of figures; one the Storyteller didn't hold so close to her chest.

The pair of hunting brothers were happy to oblige him, sharing his views when it came to higher powers.

Fuck them.

Let them play in their little castles and call themselves gods. Marcus knew of them, respected those who followed them, but when those pompous pricks started to close in on him, demanding his faith like it was expected, all bets were off.

Marcus sneered to himself. There was one in particular he wanted to give a good kick of reality to.

The Storyteller.

She was a purist, and wanted the stories to remain. Keep the powerful play going on script, which was fine. Marcus wasn't against that part.

It was when she refused to listen to those who had to live in those stories, day after day, when she refused to let them think, feel, breathe, in their own way, show who they could be beyond the walls of their inked cages…well.

That's why he left the Guild. Left her.

Why he started the Fans. To finally,

finally,

let new stories be told, or to let old ones have a chance to grow beyond their inked limits.

As Caroline returned to HQ, he wondered if this was the chance they had been waiting for.

He hoped, for everyone's sake, that the kid was right.

All for one.....

Athos was just disappointed.

The Cardinal's men never seemed to get any better.

He thought this as his sword cut through one of the guards like butter, sending the man and his red cloak to the ground.

He turned, only to face a gold mask.

Of course.

The Guild.

They always slipped in whenever a Telling happened, blending in to make sure the story was on track.

Athos groaned internally. He raised his sword, and they were off.

At least, he thought as he blocked the sword going for his heart, *it will be more of a challenge.*

Swiping it away, he made eyes at Porthos who had just used his crossbow to take down ten men at once.

Showoff, Athos thought fondly.

Porthos spied the golden mask he was fighting and grinned ferally. He was not a fan of the Guild either.

Barreling over, he whipped out his gun, aiming for the ankles.

Can't send them back dead, unfortunately. That'd give them away.

The **crack** of the gun sent the Guildsman to the ground, groaning.

At this point, Rochefort growled and ordered his men back as usual.

Coward, Athos thought triumphantly as Porthos, Aramis, and d'Artagnan came toward him.

A flash of red light, bright as the Aurora Athos had

never seen, streaked across the sky.

The narrative was over for now.

The Three Musketeers (*four*, Athos corrected to himself as his eyes strayed to d'Artagnan, *he's earned it at this point*) vanished back to the Scrapyard into a flash of golden light.

After blinking the spots from their eyes, they slipped over to the local pub, being greeted with nods and free wine.

Porthos is in the middle of one of his tales when a hush falls over the crowd.

A man clad in black, trailing static behind him, has entered the pub.

Everyone looks to the four at the back.

Athos waves his hand. Aramis murmurs something to his God.

Hopefully asking if something interesting will finally happen.

The black clad figure walks to their table and takes the last seat.

Athos sips his drink. "Hello, Marcus."

Marcus removes his hood, a bright smile on his face.

"Gentlemen. I think I finally have a proposition for you. What would you say to a proper fight for once?"

Athos looked to the others, feral smiles piercing the air.

Athos gives his best sardonic grin.

"It's about time. We're listening."

What's in a name

Rumple was not exactly pleased.

The fair Storyteller had barged right into his home in the forest outside the Scrapyard.

During his downtime between Tellings no less.

A time he held sacred considering the… distinct opinions the rest of the inhabitants of his story had about him.

He put on his best smile and bowed. "My lady, fair Storyteller, what can a humble…"

"Save your groveling, Stiltskin. I have a task for you when you are not doing a Telling."

Rumple's eyes widened and he straightened. "Of course, my lady. How may I be of service?"

The Storyteller's eyes, usually calm and distant like one in a daydream, were now alert like a wolf on the hunt.

"The Fans have risen again. They have had contact with the Musketeers and Juliet Capulet."

Rumple hid his shock well. The Fans have tried to martial forces before, grabbing what figures they had loved to grovel over before their recruitment to the Fans' ranks.

But they have never dared touch the classics. Those stories were too well-watched.

"They have gotten bolder," Rumple commented. The Storyteller glared.

"They've gotten reckless," she snarled, beginning to pace the room, "Those brats have tried to belittle my power before, but this, this is…"

War, Rumple thought. He dared not speak it though. Words have far too much power here in the Scrapyard.

The Storyteller stopped pacing and looked back at him. "I need you to keep an eye on those they have already recruited. Remind them why it's…. not wise to break my laws. Also, I need you to get in touch with your contacts. Make sure they can't get close to anyone else."

Rumple simply nodded, bowing again.

"Of course, my Lady."

Rumple's mind wandered as the Storyteller began to leave.

Which is why he didn't notice until it was too late that she had stopped, her cherry lips turning into a vicious smirk.

Pain.

As sudden as a thunderclap, Rumple was doubled over, grabbing his sides and head, the lines of his story screaming like banshees, the shadows allowed to play him like a cheap violin.

Rumplestil…..
Rumplestilt……

Name....

Namenamenamename.......

Rumple's cry of agony shattered the peace around him, the birds flying for cover.

Then, blessed numbness as the shadows were batted back.

Cherry lips against his ear.

"Don't fail me, Stiltskin. The price of failure cannot be bought with woven gold."

With that, the Storyteller was gone.

Leaving Rumple on the ground, grumbling to himself.

No matter what his story claimed, he was as much a slave to a debt

as

the

rest.

Forget me not

Juliet walked through the Scrapyard, the note tucked
into her pocket, jaw set.

The streets blurred by her, each one leading to an-
other paper tower full of its own stories.

Finally, she got to the apartment.
Knocking on the door with shaking hands,
and then

f

a

l

l

i

n

g

right into his arms.

Romeo checked the hall, then ushered her inside.
A sweet kiss passed between them as easy as a hello.

Juliet pulled away.
She held up the note.

Romeo sighed.
"They contacted you?"

Juliet nodded.
Romeo sighed again, connecting their foreheads.
He had heard of these Fans, heard of what they had
tried to do.

He knew that now, time was limited for them.
Then again, that wasn't new for them, considering.

Romeo looked to his Juliet, drinking in the sight of
her like he did every time he died. .

Green eyes,
			freckled nose,
						mole next to her ear.

Each thing burned into his memory, better than any
token or forget-me-not.

Romeo kissed her again, feet stumbling deeper into the apartment.

He wanted to memorize every part of her before everything became too much, before he begged her not to wander too far from him though he knew she must, much like every time those cursed lines begun.

She had wandered away from him, heartbroken but strong, so many times and had come out the other side.

Who was he to argue with something like that?

By the end of that eternal afternoon, Juliet left, head held high like always, though now that determination was not diluted with exhaustion.

Dagger at her hip, note clutched in her hand.

She wandered into the darkened alley that some said didn't exist
(an odd thing to say, in a world of fictions and tales,)
and spoke to the dark.

"How can I help?"

From the shadows, static danced.

A Dilemma

Rumple shook his head as he kept his eyes on their base

in the quieter part of the Scrapyard.

Foolish, the lot of them.

Going out and brandishing their might by recruiting a Shakespeare

when the Storyteller is actively gunning for them?

What kind of idiots were they?

"The idiots you supported for a while."

Rumple groaned. Marcus.

Turning from his hiding spot, Rumple plastered on a smile.

"Nice to see an old friend, as always."

Marcus quirked a brow. "You're a bit far from home."

Rumple shrugged. "It's good to get fresh air now and again."

"You're spying for her."

Rumple had too much dignity to deny it.

Marcus sighed and pinched the bridge of his nose. "Look, I know we've had this conversation before. You realize how much happier…."

"Spare me the lecture. The facts are now as they were before: this is suicide, anyone working with you will get Erased, swallowed by those damned shadows that she plays pet with, end of story, literally. Just like……"

He didn't finish.

Marcus just looked at Rumple for a moment.

"Aren't you tired?"

Rumple was taken aback for a moment before smoothing over his features.
"Of what?"

"Of being afraid. Of living the same damn story over and over again?"

"And what would you have us do again? Keep those tales locked away?"

"I'd have us be free to tell other stories, other renditions of who they may be besides what we know."

"Yes, because the Storyteller…."

"She, for all her power, is a lot like you, you know."

Rumple suddenly felt a lump in his throat.

Marcus knelt to be at eye level with the man.

He placed a hand on his shoulder.
"Both of you are cautious, afraid of the unknown. I understand caution. But living your whole life with

your head down, never moving forward, has to get tiring after so long."

Rumple shrugged him off. "We all have our vices. Even the paragons among us."

Marcus gave a sardonic smile and rose.
"Yes, but isn't that the point of those stories? To rise above them?"

Rumple gave a humorless laugh.
"Mine ends as more of a fall than a rise."

Marcus nodded, conceding to his point. He started to leave, then stopped.
Turned.
"It doesn't have to be."

Rumple gave another bitter laugh.

Marcus shrugged, his expression simply saying,
think about it
before vanishing in a flash of static, air crackling after him.

Rumple shook his head.

Foolish, the lot of them.

(That didn't stop Marcus's words from ringing true in his ears.

After all, the foolish are sometimes the wise in disguise.)

The Erased

Down below
in the

Q   U   I   E   T

bowels of the Scrapyard
live the lost,
the faded,
the forgotten.

These souls were once
stories that tickled the ears.
Whose rhymes lived on everyone's lips,
who were once Gods.

Mindless in their loneliness
desperately tearing at their sealed
mouth,
ears,
and eyes.
They have voices
but nothing to scream.

Just lamentations that would
fall on deaf ears anyway.
They are myths
lost to that conqueror we
call time.
They are burned books,
hushed folklore,
lost histories.

They clutch themselves
as their own stories
tear them to shreds
like vultures
over
a
corpse.

They are swallowed and tormented by shadows
that obey no one.
They are only held back by *HER*

Barely, just barely
But I let them out to play when it is needed
When it is necessary.

You would expect a hellish
CLATTER
to rule this darkened world.

Oh, naïve reader.
Don't you know the
worst punishment for a story
is
eternal
silence?

Scream

There were days when she wanted to scream.
Run as fast as she could
toward a clearing,
a crowd,
something.

She wanted to scream how her story
was not just some small cautionary tale
people told children
to remind them to stay away
from wolves with too sharp

T   E   E   T   H

and darkened forests
and lying grandmas.
She had seen the belly of the Beast.
Knew how coppery its
blood
was and how its stomach
stretched around her.
She had that Beast in her ear every

damn

time

someone started the story.

Always purring his sweet promises and delicate threats.
She wanted to scream how because of HER
(Damn witch, damn bitch, damn Storyteller!)
she never got to show the world that yes,
she actually had learned her lesson
the eternal damnation can stop now

please,
please,
PLEASE.

But no.

She could not scream, nor cry, nor even sometimes
fight back.

She was just sweet
Little
Red
Riding Hood.

And she had to keep paying for her
sin
so then no one else
had to know what it was
to want to scream and never
be heard.

Her Philosophy (Reprise)

I never wanted this.
I never wanted to become a cackling fiend
in a story I don't recognize anymore.
Yet they paint me in the colors
of the wicked and damned
to those bright-eyed followers
of theirs.

They make me seem like a tyrant.
They don't understand.
They don't get how easy it is for a story
to get tossed aside.

To get Erased, like it's nothing.
Like it never meant anything when
it meant everything to me.
They never held the broken
tale in their palms and watched it

SHATTER

into shadow and tears.

I've had to do that.
Coax them through the
terrifying moments
as rigor mortis settles in for a nap.
Yes, I can be cruel.
But they don't understand.
This is all I have.
I will defend those I love like
the countless brave warriors who
stood before Death and screamed-

NOT TODAY

If I let go, if I let them leave me
who knows how long they may last without me.

They need me.
They *need* me.
They need *me*.

These stories are my life.
And they are mine, mine, MINE.
And I, like so many mortal men who
fought,

bled,
and died for valor,
and love,
and other sweet ideals,

I
will
defend
what's
MINE.

If You Look Long Enough
into the Abyss....

Thunder rolled overhead. She paid it little mind.

Around her, the shadows thickened, swirling in patterns both hypnotizing and horrifying.

They parted, a small burst of static rippling through the room.

"Marcus," she hisses, eyes still looking to the sky.

"Storyteller."

"Finally here to get rid of me yourself?"

"No. I'm here to talk to you."

"Last I remember, you and yours aren't exactly advocates for diplomacy."

"Well, I figured this time could be an exception, considering….."

He didn't finish. He didn't have to.

She turned, a sneer distorting her once dreamlike features. "Don't do me any favors."

Marcus held his hands out, pleading.
"Please. We want the same thing. We both want to see stories thrive. But what you're doing…."

"YOU DON'T UNDERSTAND," she shouted, her voice causing the shadows to rise.

"THEY ARE ALL I HAVE, ALL THAT I AM. IF I LET THEM GO, IF I LET OTHERS DISTORT THEM, THEY WILL DIE."

"Please," Marcus begged, stepping closer, "This isn't you. They," he points to the shadows "are corrupting you. Can't you see that?"

The Storyteller didn't seem to hear him. She snarled, eyes dark and foggy, like one caught in a nightmare.

"You raise your armies, you call me a villain, then you

expect me to believe that you come with words of peace?"

The shadows shot out, pushing Marcus back. He stumbles to the floor.

"LIAR! LIAR, JUST LIKE ALWAYS," she cried.

"JUST LIKE WHEN YOU SAID FOREVER. LIAR!"

That final cry shook the Tower furiously, both stumbling.

Marcus rose, tears in his eyes.
"This ends one of two ways. You know that better than anyone."

He steps close, uncaring of the shadows around him.

He reaches out to place a hand on her cheek, but she slaps it away.

"True love's kiss won't save you," she snarled, "because you need to be in love for that."

Marcus withdraws his hand, wounded.

He closes his eyes. When they open again, they are steel.

"I'm sorry it has to end like this."

With a burst of static, he's gone.

With an anguished cry, the rain finally comes plummeting down,
the thunder striking the ground like a call to arms.

By failing to prepare.....

Caroline watched as Marcus reentered HQ.
Eyes downcast, jaw clenched.
He looked over at her.
"You were right."

Caroline didn't know how badly she wanted
to be wrong until that moment.

Now, she wished that she had swallowed the bitter words,
her attempts at convincing Marcus what he was trying
to do
was a fool's errand.

She had been so confident, so sure.
What had that brought her?
Her friend's sorrow, apparently.

Caroline walked over, laying a hand on Marcus's
shoulder.

He took a moment, then nodded, walking further into
the room

and addressing those before them.

"The Storyteller refuses to listen to reason. She has become consumed by her own desire to hold onto these stories so tightly that she chokes them to death. We have no other option but to stop her."

They all wait as Marcus pauses for the phrase they all think but he, as their self-appointed leader, is the only one able to say.

"We must do this by any means necessary."

Caroline spots Juliet's blank features melt into a twisted satisfaction.

The Musketeers remain unmoved.

The woman in red simply grins that odd, innocent grin.

The man in blue is the only one uncomfortable, crossing his arms over his red crest.

Marcus doesn't miss this, but also doesn't address it.

"Now, to begin, we need a way inside….."
"I can help with that."

Everyone's head whirls to the front door, where Rumple stands.

Marcus lifts a brow. Rumple shrugs.
"She's gone mad, simple as that. And last I checked, having a mad ruler never did anyone any good."

"So, you choose the lesser of two evils, is that it?" Juliet sneers. Rumple simply sighs.

"I chose the hill I made the decision to die on years ago. Nothing more."

Marcus simply regards this with a nod as Rumple joins them.

The plan is concocted quickly as thunder rolls overhead, displaying one message loud and clear:

There is not much time.

Of Calms and Storms

The rain thundered down from the sky.
Athos barely noticed.
His eyes were stapled to the swirling

T
   O
      W
E
   R

before him.

The comm in his ear
(clever things those were)
buzzed with static in time with the
rhythmic thunder.

"We are in position. Porthos, you're up."

A chuckle came over the comms.
"To freedom, lads!"

Indeed.
Athos slowly made his way toward the building.
Next to the front gate, the Guild had their hands full
with a
seemingly
drunk Porthos.

They never noticed him.
His hands easily undid the latch of the
concealed back gate.
Then he was inside the Tower of the Storyteller.
He had infiltrated castles before, yet today,
today,
he felt more pride than he had previously.

Sneaking quietly, he heard the roar of Porthos,
brazen as ever,
as he broke free of the Guild.
Athos quickened his pace,
Aramis popping up from the shadows
on the wings of a clap of thunder.

The Three Musketeers were ready for battle.
Athos turned a corner…

right into a group of Guild warriors, swords drawn. Athos wished for a moment he hadn't told d'Artagnan to stay behind.

Athos heard Aramis count quickly before whispering

"Sixty."

Only sixty? What a shame.

Athos drew his sword, hearing the sound of his friends doing the same.

Well, sixty would be a good start.

"All for one and one for all!"

With that, they charged.

The Plot Thickens

Everything was going according to plan.

Marcus smiled as he watched the confused guards chase and fight the Musketeers through his binoculars.

Phase one complete.

Lowering them, Marcus turned as shouts echoed around the square outside the Tower.

More of the Guild were marching their way toward the palace.

Marcus turned to the woman in red and the man in blue. "Think you can distract these guys?"

The woman in red smiled and held up a knife. "I've fought worse than these."

The man also nodded, insignia almost shining in his enthusiasm.

"Long as they don't have kryptonite."
With that, the two were off.
The woman in red darted from the alley,
her feet sending her flying across the square.

The guards were surprised by the blur,
until the leader doubled over
his side
d
r
i
p
p
i
n
g
with blood.
Their surprise shifted quickly.

They gave chase,
down the street,
across the shops,
past shocked citizens,
then

BANG!

right into that insignia.
"Now, gentlemen, that's no way to treat a lady."
The guards began to tremble in fear.
The man in blue gave a gentle, Midwest smile
as his knuckles gave a sickening

CRACK!

Marcus grinned as the guards fled.
Alarms began to sound as the Guild was mobilized.
Marcus turned toward the last group with him.
"Are you ready?"
The figures nodded.
Phase two complete.
Now onto the hard part.

Monsters and Men

They think they are so clever.
They think because they barge in here
with swords drawn and battle cries
rattling
the walls that I will surrender.

I have read enough stories of
dumb knights with magic swords and
vacant eyes.

I know that those dragons do not simply lay down
to die.

They FIGHT.

With tooth and claw
and fiery breath.

I do not have those but
that does not mean I am not a dragon
in my own right.

I rush to my shelves,
toward those old mysterious tomes
that witches have slaved and babbled to for centuries.

Cracking open the wicked spine,
I murmur the ancient words.

They spring up in front of me,
first one, then another and another.

Fur and claws,
scales and teeth,
monstrosities no man dare utter the name of.

The first howls to the moon.

The second opens its fiery maw.

The third growls with its lion head.

I grin.

"Go! Fly and destroy all that stands in your way! Find
the people in black and send them to the deepest

depths of Hell!"

The werewolf howls again and leaps from the balcony,
The wyvern takes to the air,
the chimera thundering down the stairs.

I did not want to do it.

I didn't want it to come to this.

But they gave me no choice.

They attacked my home, attacked my sanctuary
and I do not desire to lay down and die.

I don't care what I am anymore.

Victim or villain, it doesn't matter.

The hunt is on.

Houston, We Have A......

This was a problem.

Marcus dodged the wyvern as it swooped down again, nearly grabbing him.

Luckily, the man in blue flew by, grabbing it by its neck.

It roared, the two taking to the skies, fire and fists piercing the air high above.

The woman in red danced away from the werewolf, head high, knife ready.

"Bad dog," she growled, dancing away as it charged again.

Now where did the....

a low rumble sounded behind Marcus, making his hair stand on end.

He turned slowly around….
to see the cold,
HUNGRY
eyes of the chimera.

Smoke billowed from the goat's mouth, the snake dripping poison.

Static erupted around Marcus, eyes blazing with code.

He wasn't afraid of some ancient freakshow.

The two charged against each other.

Up above, there was a

CRACK!

that sounded like thunder.

The crashing body of the wyvern dispelled that idea quickly.

The man in blue flew over, crashing into the chimera.

Behind it, Caroline emerged.
She pounced upon the creature's back, the snake head in her grasp.
Twisting it, it
hissed
before a sickening **POP**!
sounded out, the snake falling limp.

Their eyes met.

"She's inside."

That's all Marcus needed to hear as his eyes trained onto the goat.

The lion against yet another strong man, history replaying like a ringing storm.

The goat tried to throw its fire, a furry wall barreling into Marcus's back.

The fire went wide, but he was pinned by canine fury.

A moment of dread.

Then the great beast ROARED
then went limp.
A knife in its back.

The woman in red smiled, triumphant.

The chimera behind him breathed its last as a
Herculean

Snap!

sounded out into the quiet square.
Marcus looked to the Tower.

He couldn't tell if their problems were over, or if they
had only begun.

Oh, Happy Dagger

Juliet took a breath as she crept through the shadows.

Around her, the *clack* and *ding* of swords rang louder than any cathedral bell.

Porthos's whoop as he happily tackled five guards at once gave her a small smile.

He was a madman, but a hell of a fighter.

Something you need when you're facing a god.

Juliet snuck further up the Tower.

A blur of blue whooshed passed a window as she slipped up the

W

    I

       N

         D

       I

     N

 G

staircase.

She heard the cry of dying beasts and the desperate
horns of the Guild.

Her hands shook as she got to the ornate door.

She hesitated.

It was odd, how fear settles in
right at the moment of freedom.

She tried not to think about how much
it felt like rigor mortis settling into her bones
(a feeling she knew all too well, too intimately to still
be sane.)

She took another breath.

In
Out
In....

her hand rested on her hip, where it lay.

She pushed open the door with her free hand.

The Storyteller stood tall, frantically scanning an old tome, shadows dancing in fury.

It's not often Juliet sees something older than her.

She murmurs a prayer as she creeps forward.

"Romeo, Oh Romeo, be with me my Romeo."

The Storyteller whips around, a growl on her lips.

Juliet raises her dagger, her only comfort for so long.

Oh, happy dagger, at last you help me.

The Storyteller lunges….
and falls, a small kitchen knife burying itself into her leg.

The two women look to see Rumpelstiltskin, a blank look in his eye.

The Storyteller growled. "Here I thought you were smarter than that."

Rumple gave a humorless smile.

"No one has ever accused me of that, my lady."

The Storyteller looked then to her doom, the
wronged woman who was no longer
an innocent girl, in love with the wrong man.

Juliet looked her in the eye, taking in the moment
she'd never admit to dreaming of.

She raised the dagger……

Take my hand.......

Marcus bounded up the stairs.
He couldn't content himself to wait.
He leaped past defeated guards,
past the Musketeers, whose furrowed brows
he paid no mind to.

Past the thundering steps of his companions behind him.
He burst through the ornate door of her study.
Juliet stands over her, dagger raised high,
determination set in her lips.
Rumple watches with blank eyes.

Marcus isn't sure what possesses him in that moment,
maybe pity,
maybe love,
maybe just simple decency,
whatever the case,
the cry of "Stop!"
leaves his lips regardless.

Juliet stops and stares at him, anger and confusion
warring on her face.

He pays her no mind.
He walks forward,
kneeling down to be eye level with her.

The Storyteller.
Marianna.

A woman he loved once upon a time.
A love that went sour
when she put on the skin of a god
and he refused to join her in her Heaven.
A love that he thought had collapsed into bitterness
but in that moment, seeing her so helpless, it rose
from the dead.

He reached out and tucked a piece of hair behind
her ear.
"This doesn't have to end this way."
She looked at him with a mix of anger and fear, the
shadow's grip still tight.
He never wanted her to look at him like that.

The trouble is, she was always a fiery woman,
stubborn to a fault.

It's why he loves her so, even now, even after all of this.
And why he can't let her die.
He thought he could, but he won't leave her to the shadows.

He stands and holds out his hand.
"Please, Marianna, let this end in a different way. Fight it."

She looked up at him, tears in her glassy, panicked eyes, the shadows whirling.
"I have to protect them. You don't understand….," the shadows
rose and fell with her panicked babbling.

Marcus leans down, a gentle smile on his face.
"I do, believe me I do. But I promise this: together, no story will ever get forgotten again."

He hears Juliet's silent fury, the man in blue's sigh of relief.
He can feel Rumple's curiosity and the woman in red's cold indifference.
He keeps his eyes on Marianna.

"Please. I know you want them to stay safe, to stay
remembered. But this,"
he gestured to the chaos around them
"isn't the way. Let us start again. Please, fight this. If
not for me, then for them,"
he gestured to the ones behind him.

To the man in blue, a modern Atlas whose strength
sometimes wasn't enough.
To the woman in red, who paid for her ignorance in
blood.
To the Musketeers, who desired new adventures.
To Rumple, whose heart may not be as cold as he
tried to portray.
To Juliet, who just wanted a life with the man she
loved.

The Storyteller saw them each anew in that moment.
The glassy look fading as she finally let go,
breaking a spell she didn't know was cast.
Sometimes a great revelation doesn't need a large
spectacle
or winding metaphors.

Sometimes they pass as easily as a breath,
quick as a smile.
Sometimes they exist in the space between two
joined hands.
The woman whose name was Marianna
swallowed her pride and tears.

She looked the man she loved once in the eye and
took
his
hand.

The shadows roared as they were batted back
to where they belonged.

Marianna looked to Marcus, a soft smile gracing her
once more dreamlike features.
"I take it back," she whispered to him. "True love's
kiss actually may work here."

Marcus gave a watery smile before testing to see if it
was true.

(It was.)

Welcome to the Story Scrapyard

She did what was needed. This was her mantra through it all.

She did what was needed when she disposed of the foolish kings of fables, all with their flaws who'd see their new world torn asunder under their reigns. They argued and schemed, stabbed each other in the back as they clawed for power, leaving their stories in shreds.

It was easy by that point to rise as a solution, heroes giving her allegiance as is their wont when evil is afoot. Together, she united them against a common threat, and they triumphed with gallantry, loyalty, and friendship.

A tale as old as time.

The Scrapyard was grateful to her, gifting her power and tower and the rest of the trappings of ruling. She, who had found this place in its darkest hour and now made it her home, forsaking the world she was born of, boring and trite in comparison. She mended the stories and made them whole again, a golden age penned by her own hand.

But she was lonely. Many forget that all the heroics in the world do not keep the cold away. So, she wrote a story of her own and willed it to be real, her heart eager for love.

She made Marcus.

Marcus, warm brown eyes and sweet smile, strong and loyal and just. She made the man of her dreams, and the people loved him. They were every storybook couple, her standing in the sun and he, happy to be at her side, supportive and sure no matter what.

Or so she assumed.

The truth was, she made him too well. Or perhaps not well enough.

He didn't see. Still doesn't see the threat, the battle is not yet won. Stories are powerful, yes, but they can die. They have died, many of them, shadows with no mouths that scream and scream and scream.

She would not let that happen to her people if she could help it. She refused to lose her kingdom, to become another fable about failed power.

Even when whispers called her controlling, cruel.

Even when those locked in tragedies begged for a respite she would not give.

Even when Marcus left her with a look of anguish because, deep down, he could not help but love her still.

She did what was needed and she will continue

to do so.

Even if it breaks her kingdom in two.

In a little world I know (Reprise)

In a little world I know
there are stories.
Stories born from a spark
so small yet so powerful
because it only takes one

B   R   E   A   T   H

to make it a flame.
Stories built on the foundation
of other stories
like a new house
built upon
an old frame.
Experience and innocence
mixing together to make something old
feel new again.
Once, there was a Storyteller
who was so scared to lose the stories
that she let other things slip from her grasp.
Love,
Mercy,

and Kindness
all crawled away
like animals who sense a coming storm,
leaving her to be swallowed by her fears and the
shadows
that made them.
It was only because of an act of defiance
followed by an act of love,
that the stories were made anew.
And a tragic curse, like always, got reversed.
The Scrapyard has always been the land of stories
but on that day an old war
finally laid down to die.
Upon its bones,
a new story emerged.
The story of Marianna, who finally accepted
that it was not on her alone to keep the stories alive.
That old stories made new do not negate the original
but give it new life, like embers reignited
upon a lucky wind.
The story of Marcus, whose hatred
for gods died because
he learned that they can be as misguided as the rest
and only need a reminder of such powerful yet

mortal things
to fall to Earth again.
A fall is not always a failure,
but sometimes it is a shift into something beautiful
and new.
A way to spread new wings to fly.
There is a reason the saying is
falling in love, after all.
A story of all those on both sides
making peace.
New adventures,
new hopes,
and new stories awaited them.
The Scrapyard, as always,
went on telling its tales
but now static and ink
mixed and merged
creating new Tellings.
The world spun on,
shaken but undisturbed
by yet another story
reaching its conclusion.
Such things seem small
from so far away.

But my friends,
it is a thing of magnitude
when you're right in the
middle
of
it.

May all your stories have happy endings,
middles,
and starts.

The End

About the Author

Nicole Zamlout graduated from the English program at The College of New Jersey. She has had fascinations with storytelling and poetry for her whole life, and hopes by the end you find some fascination with it as well. Her first book, *All These Little Stars*, was published by Read Furiously in 2021.

Find her at instagram.com/nicole.zamlout

A Note to our Furious Readers

From all of us at Read Furiously, we hope you enjoyed our latest installment in our One 'n Done series, *Tales from the Scrapyard.*

There are countless narratives in this world and we would like to share as many of them as possible with our Furious Readers.

It is with this in mind that we pledge to donate a portion of these book sales to causes that are special to Read Furiously. These causes are chosen with the intent to better the lives of others who are struggling to tell their own stories.

Reading is more than a passive activity – it is the opportunity to play an active role within our world. The causes we support are culturally and socially conscious to encourage a sense of civic responsibility associated with the act of reading. Each cause has been researched thoroughly, discussed openly, and voted upon carefully by our team of Read Furiously editors.

To find out more about who, what, why, and where Read Furiously lends its support, please visit our website at readfuriously.com/our-causes

Happy reading and giving, Furious Readers!

Read Often, Read Well,
Read Furiously!

More in the One 'n Done Series

What About Tuesday
Adam Wilson
978-0-9965227-9-3

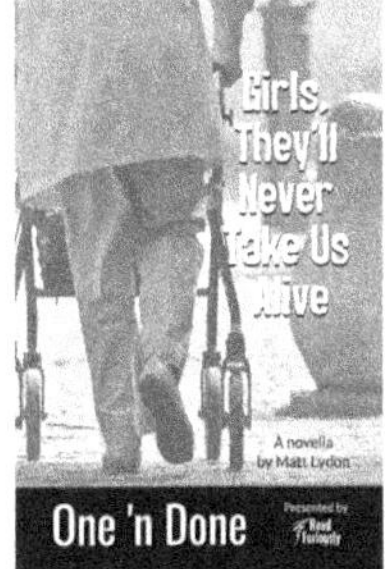

*Gurls, They'll Never Take
Us Alive*
Matt Lydon
978-1-7337360-3-9

Brethren Hollow
Bill Hemmig
978-1-7337360-8-4

Helium
Adam Wilson
and Jeff Chin
978-1-7337360-5-3

*The Legend of Dave
Bradley*
S Atzeni
978-1-7371758-8-9

The Path Home
A.J. Pelligrino
979-8-9868097-8-6

Showboi: Too Deep Too Care
Jimmy Cullen
979-8-9868097-6-2

Wund to Space
Rowan Kilduf
978-1-960869-06-7

W(h)ine & Cheese
S. Atzeni
978-1-960869-12-8

Brooklyn Family Album
Margaret Montet
978-1-960869-11-1

Tales from the Scrapyard
Nicole Zamlout
978-1-960869-18-0

The Heart Decided to Move
Melanie Bell
April 8, 2025

Small Books. Big Impact.
readfuriously.com/one

9 781960 869180